YASMIN

The Librarian

written by
SAADIA FARUQI

To Mariam for inspiring me, and Mubashir
for helping me find the right words – S.F.

To my sister, Eman, and her amazing girls,
Jana and Kenzi – H.A.

Raintree is an imprint of Capstone Global Library Limited, a company
incorporated in England and Wales having its registered office at
264 Banbury Road, Oxford, OX2 7DY – Registered company number:
6695582

www.raintree.co.uk
myorders@raintree.co.uk

Text copyright © 2022 by Saadia Faruqi.
Illustrations copyright © 2022 by Capstone.

ISBN 978 1 3982 1581 8

Editorial Credits
Editor: Kristen Mohn; Designer: Kay Fraser; Production Specialist:
Tori Abraham

Design Elements
Shutterstock: LiukasArt

British Library Cataloguing in Publication Data
A full catalogue record for this book is available from the
British Library.

Printed and bound in India

TABLE OF CONTENTS

Chapter 1
THE HELPER...5

Chapter 2
BUSY WITH BOOKS...............................10

Chapter 3
THE SPECIAL BOOK................................16

CHAPTER 1

The helper

Yasmin's class lined up to go to the library. It was the last hour of the day. Everyone was tired.

Except for Yasmin. She was excited. She had a book to show the librarian. And it was her day to be helper!

"Come in, come in!" called Mrs Kogo, the librarian. "The library is waiting for you!"

The library was big and sunny. There were shelves of books everywhere.

"Yasmin, what's that under your arm?" Mrs. Kogo asked.

"I brought my favourite book to show you. It's about cats. My baba gave it to me!" Yasmin said.

Mrs Kogo's desk was piled high with books.

"How nice! We'll look at it after our library work is done."

She smiled at Yasmin.

"I see that you're my helper today. If we work together, we can put all the books back in no time!"

Yasmin nodded. "I'm ready to work!"

CHAPTER 2

Busy with books

Mrs Kogo showed Yasmin how to put the books in the right place.

"The storybooks go in order by the author's last name," Mrs Kogo said. She showed Yasmin the alphabet signs on the shelves. "As long as you know your ABCs you'll be fine."

Yasmin piled all the books on a trolley and began shelving. A, then B, then C . . . all the way up to Z. She even found an author with the last name Ahmad, just like her!

Emma walked up. "Yasmin, I can't find the book I want," she complained.

Yasmin checked the author's last name. It started with a G.

"Right there!" Yasmin pointed.

"Thanks, Yasmin!" Emma said.

When the books were all put away, Mrs Kogo asked Yasmin to tidy up the tables and chairs.

Ali needed help too.

"Yasmin, do you know where

the bookmarks are?" he asked.

Yasmin found the box on Mrs

Kogo's desk. "Here you go!"

Finally, all Yasmin's tasks were finished. Now she could show Mrs Kogo her special book.

But . . . where was it? Yasmin realized she didn't have it any more.

"My kitaab!" She felt like crying. Where was her book from Baba?

CHAPTER 3

The special book

Yasmin took a deep breath and looked around. She'd worked in so many places in the library. How would she find her book? She would have to go back to each one and look.

First, she went to Mrs Kogo's desk. The box of bookmarks was there, but no special book.

Then she went to the shelves. She checked each section, A to Z. No special book there, either.

Oh no! Had someone

accidentally taken it?

Suddenly, Yasmin heard
Mrs Kogo's voice. She was
talking about animals.

Yasmin turned. Her class was sitting on the carpet. Story time had started. Mrs Kogo was reading Yasmin's special book from Baba!

She hurried towards them and found a seat next to Emma.

"Yasmin, this book is fantastic," Emma whispered. "Cats are so cool!"

"I know," Yasmin whispered back with a smile.

Soon, the bell rang. Mrs Kogo stopped reading. "Thank you for sharing this book with the class, Yasmin!"

"But we didn't get to finish it!" Ali said.

"I have an idea," Yasmin said. "I'll let Mrs Kogo borrow my book for the week. Then everyone will have a chance to read it!"

Mrs Kogo smiled. "You make a great librarian, Yasmin!"

Think about it, talk about it

* What special item might you take to school for show-and-tell or to share with a friend or teacher? Why is it special to you?

* Have you ever lost something important? If you were Yasmin in this story, what would you have done? Imagine what might have happened if Yasmin couldn't find her book.

* Have you ever been asked to help a teacher with tasks, like Mrs Kogo asked Yasmin to do? How did this make you feel? Think of a time when helping was fun. Think of another time when helping was not fun. Why were they different?

Learn Urdu with Yasmin!

Yasmin's family speaks both English and Urdu. Urdu is a language from Pakistan. Maybe you already know some Urdu words!

baba father

hijab scarf covering the hair

jaan life; a sweet nickname for a loved one

kameez long tunic or shirt

kitaab book

lassi a yogurt drink

nana grandfather on mother's side

nani grandmother on mother's side

salaam hello

shukriya thank you

Pakistan fun facts

Yasmin and her family are proud of their Pakistani culture. Yasmin loves to share facts about Pakistan!

Pakistan is on the continent of Asia, with India on one side and Afghanistan on the other.

Islamabad

PAKISTAN

The word Pakistan means "land of the pure" in Urdu and Persian.

Many languages are spoken in Pakistan, including Urdu, English, Saraiki, Punjabi, Pashto, Sindhi and Balochi.

Malala Yousafzai from Pakistan won a Nobel Peace Prize at the age of 17. She is the youngest person to win a Nobel prize.

The common leopard, snow leopard and Asiatic cheetah are three types of wild cats that live in Pakistan.

Make a Yasmin bookmark!

YOU WILL NEED:

- ruler
- thin card
- scissors
- pencil
- tracing or lightweight paper
- tape
- coloured pencils, crayons or felt tips

STEPS:

1. Cut a 4 cm x 12 cm piece of card.

2. Draw Yasmin on the card, or use the tracing paper to trace the Yasmin figure shown here.

3. If you traced, cut out your tracing and tape it to the card.

4. Use pencils, crayons or felt tips to colour Yasmin and fill in details.

5. Use your new Yasmin bookmark to save your place in your favourite book!

Saadia Faruqi is a Pakistani American writer, interfaith activist and cultural sensitivity trainer featured in *O Magazine*. She is author of two children's novels, *A Place at the Table* and *A Thousand Questions*. She is also editor-in-chief of *Blue Minaret*, an online magazine of poetry, short stories and art. Besides writing books, she also loves reading, binge-watching her favourite shows and taking naps. She lives in Houston, Texas, USA, with her husband and children.

Hatem Aly is an Egyptian-born illustrator whose work has been published all over the world. He currently lives in beautiful New Brunswick, Canada, with his wife, son and more pets than people. When he is not dipping cookies in a cup of tea or staring at blank pieces of paper, he is usually drawing, reading or daydreaming. You can see his art in books that earned multiple starred reviews and positions on the *NYT* Best-Sellers list, such as *The Proudest Blue* (with Ibtihaj Muhammad & S.K. Ali) and *The Inquisitor's Tale* (with Adam Gidwitz), a Newbery Honor winner.

Join Yasmin on all her adventures!